Easter Bonnet Bug-A-Boo

A Scratch & Sniff Story

Adapted by Krista Tucker
Based on the episode written by Andy Guerdat
Illustrated by the Disney Storybook Art Team

HARPER FESTIVAL

An Imprint of HarperCollinsPublishers

Copyright © 2020 by Disney Enterprises, Inc.
All rights reserved. Manufactured in China.
No part of this book may be used or reproduced in any manner whatsoever without written permission except
in the case of brief quotations embodied in critical articles and reviews. For information address
HarperCollins Children's Books, a division of HarperCollins Publishers, 195 Broadway, New York, NY 10007.
www.harpercollinschildrens.com

ISBN 978-0-06-284380-7

19 20 21 22 23   LEO   10 9 8 7 6 5 4 3 2 1   ❖ First Edition

Ooh la la! It's Easter! My friends and I are making bonnets. That's a fancy word for hats.

We use ribbon, feathers, and glue. Plus I brought chocolate Easter eggs for snacking. Don't they smell delicious?

Suddenly, I get an idea. "Let's have a contest to see who has the best bonnet!" I say.

"Yeah!" says Bree. "Mrs. Devine can be the judge."

"Whoever wins can lead our Easter parade," says Lionel.

I fancy up my bonnet with lots of *accoutrements*. That's French and fancy for bits and pieces.

Voilà! My bonnet is more than beautiful—it's breathtaking!

"Wow, Nancy! Good job!" says Rhonda.

"Yeah! Who has a bonnet better than that?" asks Bree.

"Hi everyone," says Grace as she rides up on her bicycle. Everyone gushes over her *très* fancy bonnet.

"Oh this old thing," she says. "It's new. It has real artificial flowers. My mom bought it for me."

Sacrebleu! Oh no! I can't believe it. Grace's bonnet is fancier than mine!

If my hat isn't the fanciest, then I won't win the contest.

Then I get an idea that's simply *magnifique*! That's French
for magnificent.
I'll get some help from Mother Nature and use real flowers!

Bree and I hurry to Mrs. Devine's house. She has the most beautiful white roses we've ever seen . . . or smelled!

"May we please use some of your flowers for our bonnets?" I ask.

"Of course, girls," Mrs. Devine says.

"*Ooh la la!* These purple flowers are gorgeous!" I say.

"Those are LiLacs. Don't they smell wonderful?" says Mrs. Devine. "But I wouldn't recommend them. Their strong fragrance tends to attract bugs."

Bugs? Yuck! I pick some daffodils instead.

Bree takes some moonflowers. "They bloom when the sun goes down," she tells me.

"*Merci*," we tell Mrs. Devine. That's French for thank you.

Bree and I add the flowers to our bonnets.

I am almost one hundred percent positive that my bonnet is much fancier than Grace's now.

But then I see Grace. She made her bonnet fancier too!
"I can't wait to lead the parade," says Grace. "See you at the contest!"

Now I need an even fancier bonnet. I follow my nose
back to Mrs. Devine's garden, and I see a butterfly. That
gives me a fantastic idea!

I need to hurry because the contest is about to start. It's a lovely spring day. Even the **trees** smell wonderful.

"I'm going to get a butterfly to land on my bonnet," I tell Bree.

"How are you going to get a butterfly to stay on your bonnet?" Bree asks.

"You'll see!" I say.

I arrive at the contest.
"Wow! Nancy's bonnet has a real butterfly on it!" says Lionel.
"Now that's fancy!" says Rhonda.

"*Merci*," I say. "Butterflies adore lilacs. That's why it's staying on my bonnet."

I feel elated. That's fancy for really happy. Even Grace's bonnet isn't as fancy as mine!

Then a honey bee flies near me. Then a ladybug . . . and then a dragonfly. "Shoo! Get away!" I say.

"You knew those flowers attracted bugs," Bree tells me.

This is unbearable! Which is fancy for I can't take it.
I run! I hide! I toss off my bonnet!

"Are you okay, Nancy?" Bree asks.

"*Oui*, yes," I say. "I guess I lost the contest. But at least I got rid of the bugs."

Then the flowers on Bree's bonnet bloom. It's sublime! That's fancy for really beautiful.

"They are MOONFLOWERS," Bree tells everyone. "They bloom when the sun starts to set, so I figured that'd be about when the parade starts. Don't they smell incredible?"

"Bree wins the contest!" says Mrs. Devine.
"Hooray! Bree will lead the parade!" we all shout.

Happy Easter, everyone!